Poptropica®

ISLAND CREATOR KIT

by Mitch Krpata

Poptropica®

An Imprint of Penguin Group (USA) Inc.

Photo credits: #2 pencil (cover, page 1), colored pencils (cover), compass (cover, page 1), eraser (cover, page 1), graph paper (cover, interior), green checkered cutting board (cover), masking tape (page 8–9), mechanical pencil (cover), notebook (cover, page 1), old paper texture (interior), red and green paperclips (interior), ripped graph paper (page 1, 6–7), rolled paper (cover), scissors (cover), T square ruler (cover, page 1), wooden surface (cover, page 1, 6–7), yellow graph paper (page 2), yellow lined notepad (page 8–9), yellow lined ripped paper (page 3) © iStockphoto/Thinkstock.

ISBN 978-0-448-46493-0

10 9 8 7 6 5 4 3 2 1

ALWAYS LEARNING

PEARSON

A Note from the Poptropica Creators

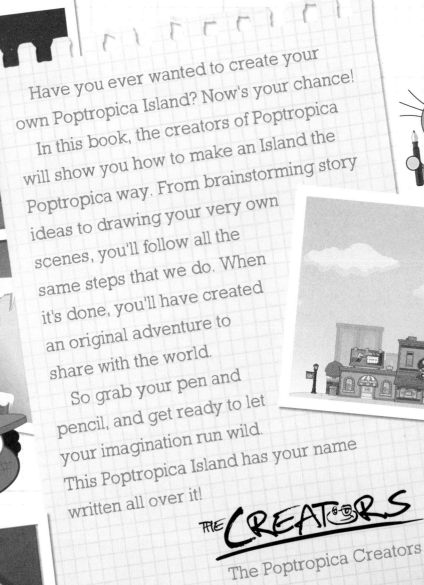

Have you ever wanted to create your own Poptropica Island? Now's your chance! In this book, the creators of Poptropica will show you how to make an Island the Poptropica way. From brainstorming story ideas to drawing your very own scenes, you'll follow all the same steps that we do. When it's done, you'll have created an original adventure to share with the world.

So grab your pen and pencil, and get ready to let your imagination run wild. This Poptropica Island has your name written all over it!

THE CREATORS

The Poptropica Creators

Write the Perfect Pitch

Every Island starts with a simple idea—what we call the "pitch." In one or two sentences, we lay out our vision for the Island. For example . . .

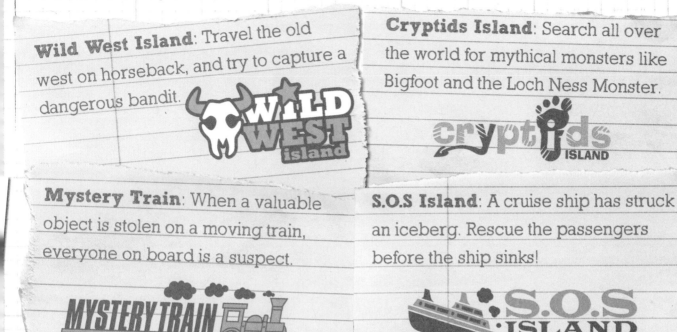

Wild West Island: Travel the old west on horseback, and try to capture a dangerous bandit.

Cryptids Island: Search all over the world for mythical monsters like Bigfoot and the Loch Ness Monster.

Mystery Train: When a valuable object is stolen on a moving train, everyone on board is a suspect.

S.O.S Island: A cruise ship has struck an iceberg. Rescue the passengers before the ship sinks!

It's your turn to make a pitch. What are your ideas for new Islands?

Get Started in Style

Before we design our characters and scenes, we draw an image that sets the look for the entire Island. This tells us if our Island is set in space. Or underwater. Or in the future. Everything else we design will be based on this. Yours can be anywhere, any time, or any style that you can imagine. So, what will your Island look like? Explore different ideas until you find one you love.

Put Yourself on the Map

You have a great idea for your Island. But in order for anyone to start playing it, they'll need to know how to get there. How will your Island appear on the map?

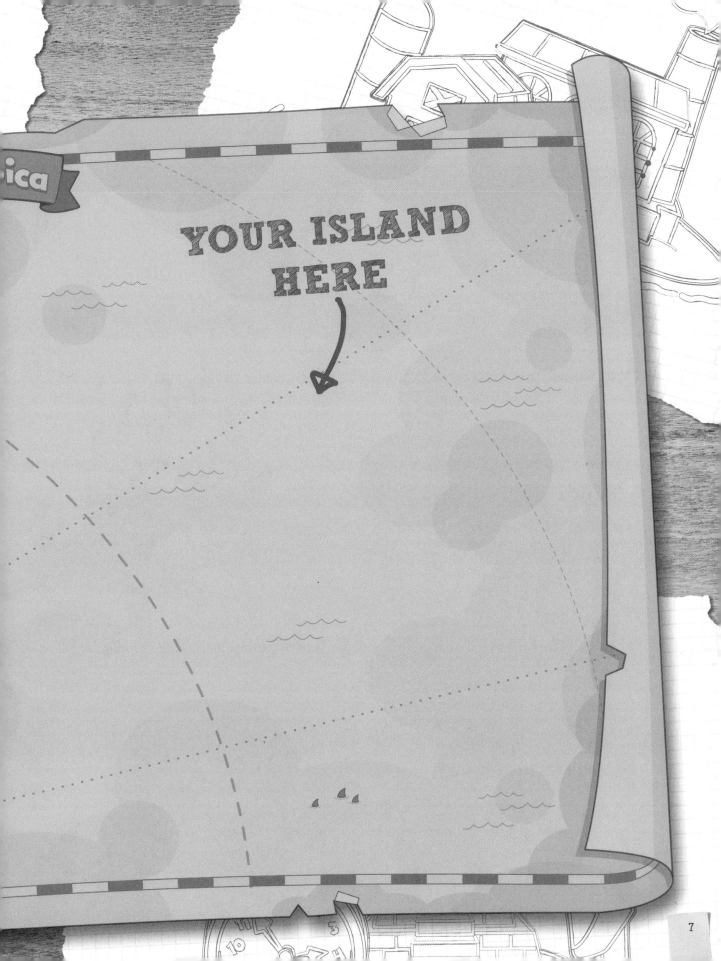

YOUR ISLAND HERE

Turn Your Pitch into Reality

Now, let's turn your pitch into an outline. Your outline doesn't need to include every detail, but it should answer the most important questions about your Island's story.

Mythology Island Outline

MYTHOLOGY island

Where does the story take place?
Ancient Greece

What problem will players need to solve?
Find the five sacred items

What characters will help players?
Aphrodite, Athena, Hades, Hercules, Poseidon

What characters will try to stop players?
Cerberus, Hydra, Zeus

What kinds of challenges will players face?
Get lost in the Labyrinth, swim to an underwater cave, climb Mount Olympus

Will players get any special powers or abilities?
Use Hades's crown to grow big and Poseidon's trident to zap Zeus

Outline

Where does the story take place?

What problem will players need to solve?

What characters will help players?

What characters will try to stop players?

What kinds of challenges will players face?

Will players get any special powers or abilities?

Go with the Flow

We make a chart of every Island that shows how a player will move through the quest from beginning to end. It doesn't have any finished art—just the names of the scenes and how they fit together.

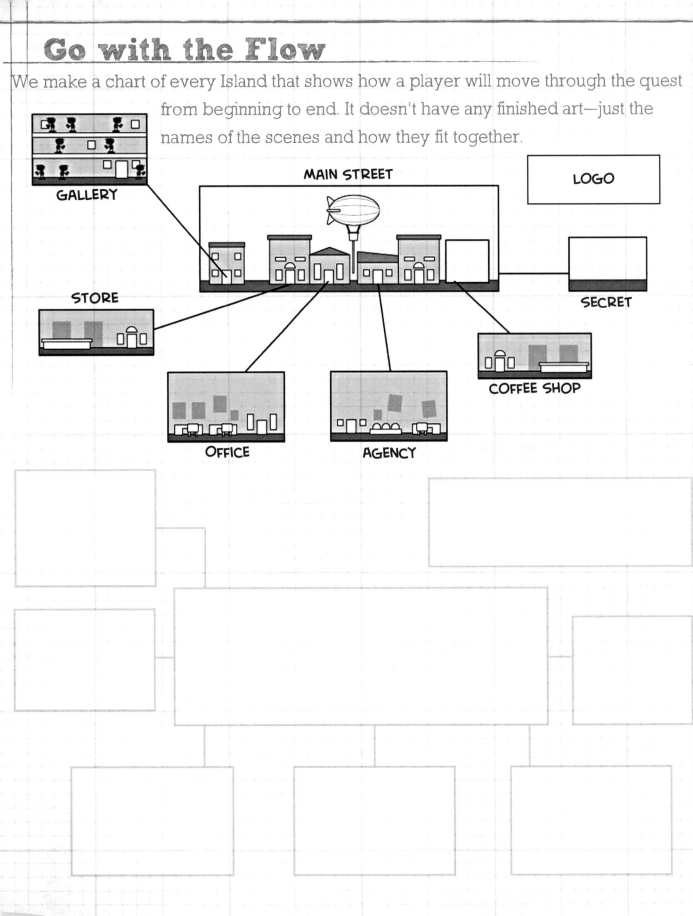

GALLERY

MAIN STREET

LOGO

STORE

SECRET

COFFEE SHOP

OFFICE

AGENCY

Try drawing your chart below. Keep in mind all the different places you want your players to go and what challenges they might find when they get there. (It's a good idea to use a pencil for this, since you may want to go back and change it later!)

Welcome to Main Street

The first thing that someone will see when they land on your Island is Main Street, so it's important to make a good first impression! Draw the buildings, signs, and landmarks that people will see when they visit your Main Street.

You can use the guides below to help you get started, or feel free to get creative and build your Main Street from scratch.

Create Your Cast of Characters

Every Poptropica Island has people who need help, from the sad pilgrims of Early Poptropica to the terrified villagers of Vampire's Curse Island. Who are the characters who live on your Island? What kind of trouble are they in?

PILGRIM   HELEN HIKER   PORTER   LASSIE LASO   SIR GAWAIN   MARK TWAIN   CHEF JEFF

Visualize Your Villain

A good story needs a great villain. Think about who your bad guys are: the evil schemes they've concocted, what makes them scary, and what their weaknesses might be. Don't be afraid to make your villains as wild and outrageous as you can imagine!

EL MUSTACHIO

BLACK WIDOW

GRETCHEN GRIMLOCK

BETTY JETTY

BINARY BARD

CAPTAIN CRAWFISH

DIRECTOR D

DR. HAR

Introduce Your Hero

Poptropica is nothing without the star of the show: you! Design your Poptropican hero for this Island. What special clothes or items will you need to make it through your adventure safely?

Pick Your Powerups

Lots of Poptropica Islands require players to master special abilities in order to win—like the Grappling Bowtie on Spy Island or the power of flight on Super Power Island. What new and exciting skills will players need to learn on your Island?

Start the Adventure!

It's time for the player to leave the safety of Main Street and begin to explore your Island. You get to decide what they'll find there. Monsters? Booby traps? Mazes?

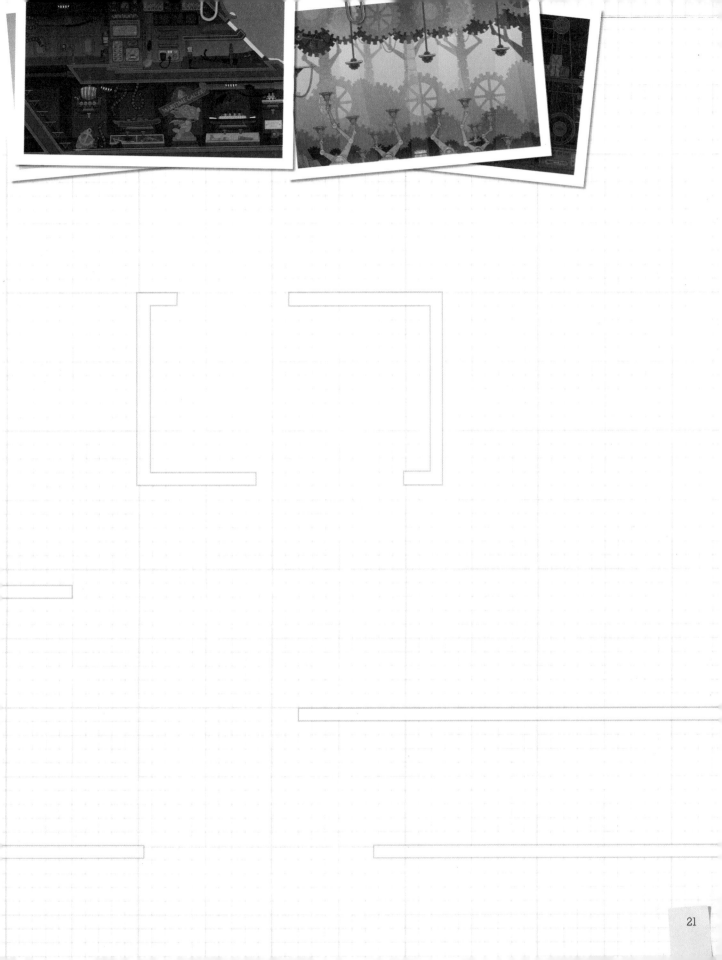

Pack Your Knapsack

Along the way, players will discover items to help in their quest. They might find the key to a locked door, a treasure to trade with a friendly character, or a clue that helps solve a mystery. Finding and using items is one of the most important parts of a Poptropica Island. What items will players find on your Island? What are they used for?

Ultra Vision Goggles

With these goggles you can see invisible lasers.

PUT ON

CLASSIC FLAVOR
POPGUM

FREE

Press SPACEBAR to blow bubbles.

CHEW

Super Villain Files

VILLAINS

TOP SECRET!

Top secret information on the escaped super villains.

EXAMINE

Build the Challenge

Don't let players get cocky! You've got some more surprises in store for them. Draw another scene, and make this one even more challenging than the last. Try to give players clues that will help them figure out how to advance.

Test Your Wits

An Island adventure isn't all action. Sometimes players need to stop and think their way through a problem. What are some puzzles that players will have to solve on your Island? They might have to memorize a pattern, put together a picture, break a code—anything you can think of. Try to stump your players!

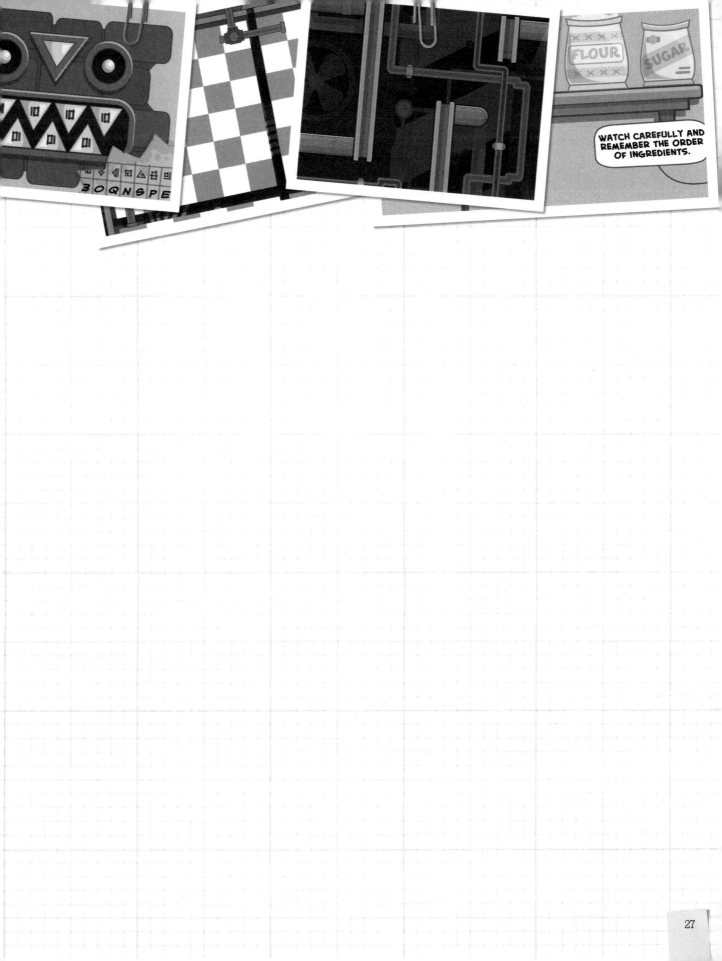

Pull Out All the Stops

Almost there! By now, your players should have a good idea of their goals and how to achieve them. But you don't want to let them off too easily. Design one more level for players to complete with as many challenges and puzzles as you can imagine.

The Grand Finale

At last—the final showdown! This might be a fight against the villain, a big chase, or a surprising plot twist. Your entire Island adventure has been leading up to this moment, so make it spectacular!

Go for the Gold

We like to think that completing a quest on Poptropica is its own reward. Just in case we're wrong, we also give a shiny gold Medallion to every player who finishes an Island.

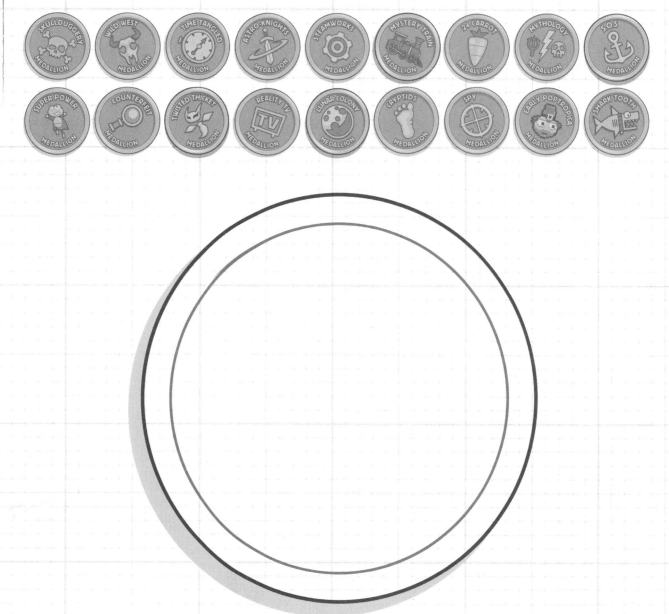

Congratulations! You've just created your own Poptropica Island. Now it's time for the best part: sharing your creation with the world. When you show off your new Island to your friends and family, you'll probably discover something that we already know—the only thing better than finishing your latest Island is starting the next one!